The
HUNTER

Paul Geraghty

RED FOX

For
O Serene One Sissons

The
HUNTER

Paul Geraghty

A Red Fox Book

Published by Random House Children's Books
20 Vauxhall Bridge Road, London SW1V 2SA

A division of Random House UK Ltd
London Melbourne Sydney Auckland
Johannesburg and agencies throughout the world

1 3 5 7 9 10 8 6 4 2

First published by
Hutchinson Children's Books 1994

Red Fox edition 1996

Printed in Hong Kong

RANDOM HOUSE UK Limited Reg. No. 954009

ISBN 0 09 966631 6

In the early morning, Jamina went with her grandfather to collect honey. They followed the honey bird far into the bush.

'I want to see elephants!' Jamina cried. 'Grandfather, do you think we will?'

'You'll be lucky,' said the old man. 'We don't see many now. Not since the hunters came.'

'Hunters!' Jamina's eyes lit up. 'I'm going to be a hunter.'

Jamina played hunters. She shot the mighty elephant; she tracked a rhino deep into the forest; she stalked a pride of lions.

Then she turned back to look for her grandfather. But she had wandered too far into the bush and the old man and the honey bird were nowhere to be seen.

She called out but there was silence.

Then, far away on the wind, Jamina heard a sound. A sad and desperate cry that tugged at her heart. She held her breath and listened.

Jamina looked up. Vultures hung high in the heavy noon heat, and all around she could sense danger.

'Never go alone into the bush,' her parents had warned. But the sound was so mournful she couldn't help but follow.
Further and further she went …

Jamina stood up and walked a few steps. The baby followed, tottering weakly in the blazing heat. Then the rain came and, cooled by the water, the elephant found strength to go on. At times they slipped and struggled, but they kept on walking, right through the storm.

As the skies cleared, the baby grew excited and for a moment Jamina thought she could hear elephants. But when she stopped to listen there was only the whispering of the wind in the grass. For a long time the elephant would not move. Then, sadly and silently, he carried on.

'If you are lost,' her grandfather had told her, 'follow the afternoon herds; they will lead you to the river. Home is on the other side.'

Jamina and the elephant set off again, but soon the baby began to slow down.

'Just a little further,' begged Jamina. But he was too tired to go on. As Jamina waited with him, she thought of her mother. If only she could call her. Soon people would worry; soon they would come searching. The baby whimpered. She stroked him gently. He had no mother to call.

'Listen!' Jamina hushed the elephant. They could hear voices. My parents! she thought.

But the dark shadows in the distance were not her parents.

'Poachers!' she gasped under her breath. Now Jamina felt she too was one of the hunted. She prayed that the baby would not whimper. But the elephant sensed evil and stayed as still as a stone until the danger passed.

Darkness fell and the whoops and howls of the night creatures sent
a shiver down Jamina's spine. She huddled close to the baby, then
clung to him in fear as the deep and terrifying groan of something
hungry sounded nearby.

As Jamina waited to be hunted, the words of her grandfather
came to her again.

'If ever you are in danger,' he had said, 'never lose hope.'

So Jamina listened for her parents. She closed her eyes and
wished for them.

But instead she saw elephants. Her mind was filled with the great herds of long ago. The mighty tuskers her grandfather had seen when he was young. Giant elephant shadows moving like ghosts across the plains.

She could hear their deep and gentle murmurs close by.

When she opened her eyes, there were elephants all around, as if she'd called them in her dream. Jamina wasn't afraid.

'Take this little one,' she said. 'And keep him safe.'

By the first light of dawn, Jamina's mother found her sleeping in the grass.

'I was playing hunters and I got lost,' Jamina said. She stayed very close to her mother all the way home.

'I will never be a hunter,' she said softly to herself as they reached the village.